The Case of the
Sweaty Bank Robber

THIRD-GRADE DETECTIVES #9

The Case of the Sweaty Bank Robber

by
George E. Stanley
illustrated by
Salvatore Murdocca

SCHOLASTIC INC.

New York Toronto London Auckland Sydney
Mexico City New Delhi Hong Kong Buenos Aires

No part of this publication may be reproduced, stored in a retrieval system, or transmitted in any form or by any means, electronic, mechanical, photocopying, recording, or otherwise, without written permission of the publisher. For information regarding permission, write to Simon & Schuster Books for Young Readers, Simon & Schuster Children's Publishing Division, 1230 Avenue of the Americas, New York, NY 10020.

ISBN   0-439-77433-0

12 11 10 9 8 7 6 5   12 13 14 15 16/0

Printed in the U.S.A.   40

First Scholastic printing, April 2005
Designed by Lisa Vega
The text of this book was set in 12-point Lino Letter.

*To all the third-grade students and teachers at
Almor West Elementary School in Lawton, Oklahoma.
You're a source of inspiration to me.*

Chapter One

"Here's your T-shirt, Todd," Noelle Trocoderro said. "We're supposed to wear them when we're working."

Todd Sloan took the T-shirt and looked at it. On the front it read I GAVE BLOOD TODAY. "I'm not giving away any of my blood!" he said.

"Don't worry. We're too young to give blood," Noelle told him. "We just have to give away orange juice."

"I don't want to wear this, Noelle," Todd said. "It's too cold for T-shirts."

"Just put it on over your regular shirt," Noelle said.

"Why do we have to do this, anyway?" Todd complained. "I don't even like to *talk* about blood. It makes me dizzy."

"Because my parents are in charge of the local blood drive, that's why," Noelle said. "They asked me to help, and I volunteered you."

Todd let out a big sigh. "Okay," he said.

"But hurry!" Noelle said. "We're already late."

Todd quickly pulled the T-shirt on over his regular shirt and then put on his heavy coat.

When Noelle and Todd got to their school, they saw a big sign in front of the gymnasium. It read COME INSIDE! WE WANT YOUR BLOOD!

"Yuck!" Todd said.

"That was my dad's idea," Noelle said.

Just as they reached the door, a man wearing a black cape came outside. His face was painted white, and when he opened his mouth, he had sharp teeth.

Todd stopped. "Who is that?" he whispered.

"My dad," Noelle said. "He thought it would be funny if he dressed up like Dracula."

"Hey! You're late!" Mr. Trocoderro said. "You're supposed to be giving people orange juice!"

"Sorry, Dad," Noelle said.

She and Todd hurried inside.

All around the gymnasium, there were people lying on padded tables. They had needles in their arms.

"I can't look at this, Noelle," Todd whispered.

"Then close your eyes and hold on to my arm until we get to the refreshment table," Noelle whispered back.

"Okay," Todd said.

Slowly they made their way across the gym floor.

Finally Noelle said, "You can open your eyes now."

Todd opened his eyes. "This is really creepy, Noelle," he said. "Why do they need so much blood, anyway?"

"Mom told me last night that the local blood supply is low," Noelle said. "They usually do this at the blood bank, but my parents thought more people would come if they did it at the school."

"I don't feel well," Todd said. "I'm sweating, and I'm getting sick to my stomach."

"Todd, the police see blood all the time!"

Noelle said. "If you really want to be a good Third-Grade Detective, then you're going to have to look at it sooner or later too!"

The Third-Grade Detectives was what their teacher, Mr. Merlin, called their class. They helped the police solve crimes. Mr. Merlin had a friend, Dr. Smiley, who was a police officer. Sometimes their class used the laboratory in her basement to examine evidence.

Just then Amber Lee Johnson walked up to the refreshment table. She looked at the T-shirts Noelle and Todd were wearing.

"You're not supposed to have those on," Amber Lee said.

"Why not?" Noelle demanded.

"It says that you gave blood," Amber Lee told her. "You shouldn't make people think you gave blood if you didn't."

"My parents are in charge of the blood drive, Amber Lee, and they said we should wear these T-shirts," Noelle said. "Do you want some orange juice?"

"Okay," Amber Lee said. "And a couple of cookies."

4

Noelle handed Amber Lee a cup of orange juice.

Todd gave her two cookies.

"Do you need any help here?" Amber Lee asked. "I'm really good at things like this."

Noelle shrugged. "I guess so," she said. "We may get busy later."

"Good," Amber Lee said. She looked around the room. "Where are your parents? I want to get one of those T-shirts to wear."

Noelle pointed to the other side of the gymnasium. "My mother is behind that big stack of T-shirt boxes," she said. "Talk to her."

"I'll be right back," Amber Lee said.

Noelle looked at Todd and rolled her eyes.

Just then a man stepped up to the table.

"Hello, Mr. Polk," Noelle said.

"Hello, kids," Mr. Polk said. "I'll take some of that orange juice."

Todd poured Mr. Polk a cup and handed it to him. Mr. Todd sat down in a chair next to the refreshment table.

"Whooh! I'm tired. I'm having a really busy weekend," Mr. Polk said. "I helped with the PTA

5

fund raiser yesterday, and I've been up since early this morning selling insurance."

"Thank you for giving blood today, Mr. Polk," Noelle said.

"No problem," Mr. Polk said. He took a long drink of his orange juice. "I'm always happy to stop and give away some of my blood when people need it."

Todd made a funny sound with his throat.

Mr. Polk looked at him. "What's wrong, Todd?" he said. "You look kind of pale."

"Todd gets sick if you talk about blood too much," Noelle said.

"Oh yeah, I've heard about people like that," Mr. Polk said. "It's some kind of phobia."

Noelle looked up and saw the new police chief heading toward the refreshment table. "Here comes Chief Douglas," she whispered to Todd.

When Chief Douglas reached them, he said, "How about some of that orange juice, kids?"

"Yes, sir!" Noelle said. She handed him a cup.

Suddenly Chief Douglas's walkie-talkie

squawked. "CHIEF! CHIEF! THIS IS DEPUTY RICE! WE'VE GOT A BIG PROBLEM! BOTH BANKS WERE BROKEN INTO LAST NIGHT AND ROBBED! YOU NEED TO GET HERE RIGHT AWAY!"

Chief Douglas set the orange juice down and ran out of the gym.

"Wow!" Todd said. "I can't believe that somebody robbed *both* banks."

"That's terrible!" Mr. Polk said. "I guess Chief Douglas has his work cut out for him today!"

All of a sudden Noelle had a great idea.

The Third-Grade Detectives could help Chief Douglas solve his first major case!

Chapter Two

When Amber Lee came back to the refreshment table, Leon Dennis was with her.

"Thank goodness you're here, Amber Lee!" Noelle said. "Todd and I have to take a break!"

Todd gave Noelle a funny look.

"Really?" Amber Lee said.

Noelle nodded. "I think it's the law or something," she said. "You always get a break after you've been working for a while."

Noelle looked at Leon. "Why don't you go get a T-shirt so you can help Amber Lee?" she said.

"All right!" Leon said.

"Show me what I'm supposed to do," Amber Lee said.

Noelle carefully poured some orange juice into a paper cup.

She picked it up and pretended to hand it to Todd.

"After you serve a person the orange juice, then you say, 'Thank you for giving blood today.'"

"I can do that," Amber Lee said. "People say that I have very good manners."

"Don't forget the cookies," Todd reminded her.

Leon came back wearing his "I Gave Blood Today" T-shirt. It was almost touching the floor. "Your mother only had extra, extra large," he said, "but she said if my mother washed it in really hot water, it would shrink."

"You look fine, Leon," Noelle said. "Okay, Todd and I are going to take our break. We'll be back in a few minutes."

"Don't hurry," Amber Lee said. "Leon and I have this under control."

Noelle and Todd put on their coats and headed across the gym floor toward the door.

Mr. Trocoderro was talking to someone, so he didn't notice when they left.

Outside, Todd stopped. "Why did we need to take a break?" he asked. "I'm not tired."

"I'm not either, Todd," Noelle said. "We're

going to check out those bank robberies!"

"What?" Todd said.

"I saw this great TV show last night, Todd," Noelle said. "These kids actually went to police headquarters every day after school to help the police solve crimes. They even had their own offices. I think the Third-Grade Detectives should do that too."

"Do you really think the police would let us do something like that?" Todd asked.

"Of course! Chief Douglas is new in town," Noelle said. "He needs all the help he can get."

"You're right!" Todd said. "He'll probably be happy to see us!"

The First State Bank and the First National Bank were located on the town square.

When Todd and Noelle got there, they saw police cars in front of both buildings.

"Let's check out the First State Bank first," Noelle said.

But just as they got to the front door, Deputy Rice strung some yellow tape across it. "You can't go in there," he said. "It's a crime scene."

"We know," Noelle said. "That's why we're here."

Deputy Rice gave them a puzzled look, then said, "Oh, you two are in Mr. Merlin's class, aren't you? You're some of the Third-Grade Detectives."

Noelle nodded and gave him a big smile. She reached out to open the door.

But Deputy Rice stopped her again. "You still can't go inside," he said.

"Why not?" Noelle said. "Kids can help the police solve lots of crimes."

"And since Chief Douglas is new in town, we thought we'd help him this solve this one," Todd added.

Deputy Rice grinned. "I saw that TV show too," he said. "But this is *real* life, and Chief Douglas said that *nobody* was allowed in the bank without his permission."

"Where is he now?" Noelle said. "We'll go get his permission."

"He's at the First National Bank," Deputy Rice said.

"Come on, Todd," Noelle said.

They hurried across the square to the First National Bank building.

Its door had yellow tape across it too.

There was another police officer standing in front of it.

"We need to talk to Chief Douglas," Noelle said. "It's important."

"Wait here," the police officer said.

He went inside the bank.

A few minutes later he returned with Chief Douglas.

Chief Douglas looked at Noelle and Todd. "What do you want?" he asked. "I'm very busy."

"I'm Noelle, and this is Todd. We're two of the Third-Grade Detectives," Noelle told him. "Our class knows a lot about solving—"

"I've heard all about you," Chief Douglas said, interrupting her, "and I don't think the police department will need your help anymore."

Chapter Three

Noelle and Todd watched Chief Douglas get into a patrol car and drive away.

"That makes me so mad!" Noelle said. "He acts like we're in kindergarten!"

"I know," Todd said. "I think we should tell Mr. Merlin and Dr. Smiley how Chief Douglas is treating us."

"Maybe. But now we'd better get back to the gym," Noelle said. "I don't want Amber Lee complaining to my parents that our break was too long."

Noelle and Todd hurried to the school.

There were still a lot of people going in and out of the gym. Mr. Trocoderro was greeting everyone with, "Velcome. Ve vant your blood."

When he saw Noelle and Todd, he said, "Where did you two go?"

"We took a work break," Noelle said.

"A *what*?" Mr. Trocoderro asked.

"We don't have time to explain now, Dad. We're in a hurry," Noelle said. "See you later!"

When Noelle and Todd got to the refreshment table, Amber Lee and Leon were surrounded by people wanting orange juice and cookies.

Noelle and Todd went right to work.

All of a sudden, Amber Lee looked up and said, "Where have you two been?"

Noelle gave her a puzzled look. "Here," she said. "Handing out orange juice and cookies, just like you and Leon."

"You've been so busy, you probably just didn't notice that we were back," Todd added.

Amber Lee acted like she wanted to say something else, but she didn't.

When the crowd of people at the refreshment table thinned out, Noelle said, "Amber Lee, why don't you and Leon take a break? You've worked really hard."

"That's the truth!" Amber Lee said. "Oh look, Leon! There's Dr. Smiley. Come on! We need to talk to her about the next meeting of the Dr. Smiley Fan Club."

"Noelle, we should probably talk to her about—," Todd started to say, but Noelle interrupted him with, "We'll do it later, Todd."

Todd gave her a funny look. "Why not now?" he asked.

"I've been thinking," Noelle said. "If we tell Mr. Merlin and Dr. Smiley how Chief Douglas is treating us, then they'll probably say something to him. He might change his mind and let us help the police again *because we're kids*. I want to *prove* to Chief Douglas that he needs the Third-Grade Detectives *because we're good*! I don't want him to change his mind because some adults told him he should."

"You're right," Todd said. "But how will we do it?"

"We'll find out as much about those bank robberies as we can," Noelle said.

"We'll watch television, and we'll read the newspaper.

"We'll write down everything we learn, just like the police do.

"The Third-Grade Detectives are good, Todd! We just need to make Chief Douglas believe it."

By Monday morning, Noelle and Todd had almost filled a big red tablet with information about the two bank robberies.

"Now what?" Todd asked. He and Noelle were walking to school.

"I don't know," Noelle said. "We have a lot of facts, but we don't have any suspects."

When they got to school, Todd said, "I have to give Mrs. Franklin a check for my lunch. I forgot to bring it last week."

Mrs. Franklin, Principal Jenkins's secretary, wasn't in the outer office, but Noelle heard her talking to Principal Jenkins in the principal's office.

Noelle and Todd went to the door.

Noelle could feel the heat coming out of the room.

Everyone in school knew that Principal Jenkins liked to keep her office really warm.

Mrs. Franklin and Principal Jenkins were looking at something on the wall.

Just then Mrs. Franklin moved, and Noelle saw what it was.

"Oh no!" Noelle said. "Someone blew the door off the wall safe!"

Chapter Four

Noelle and Todd stepped into the room.

"Principal Jenkins!" Noelle said. "When did that happen?"

"Sometime over the weekend, I guess," Principal Jenkins replied. "We just discovered it."

"Oh, my goodness!" Mrs. Johnson said. "What's this dirty thing doing on the floor?"

She picked up a white handkerchief and dropped it into a trash basket.

"I'm certainly glad the PTA fund raiser money wasn't in the safe, like it usually is," Principal Jenkins said.

"Where was it?" Noelle asked.

"At my house," Principal Jenkins said.

"It was late when we finished Friday night, and we were all tired, so we just counted the money, and then I took it home."

"So there's no money missing from the safe?" Noelle asked.

"No, there's . . . oh, wait!" Principal Jenkins said. "The big plastic milk jug is gone."

Todd and Noelle looked at each other.

"Milk jug?" Todd said.

"That's right," Principal Jenkins said. "The second-grade classes collected pennies for the animal shelter. They were in a big plastic milk jug."

"The thief must have been mad because there wasn't any other money in there," Mrs. Johnson said, "so he or she probably just took the pennies out of spite!" She shook her head. "What is this world coming to?"

Just then Chief Douglas and Deputy Rice arrived.

Chief Douglas frowned when he saw Noelle and Todd. "This is a crime scene, kids," he said. "You need to leave." He took off his coat. "Why is it so hot in here?" he asked.

"I like it toasty in my office," Principal Jenkins said.

Deputy Rice wiped his brow with his handkerchief. "Wow!" he said. "I'm sweating up a storm!"

Noelle and Todd left Principal Jenkins's office, but they stood outside the door to listen.

"Hey, Chief! Something interesting here," Deputy Rice said. "This safe was blown open the same way as those vaults at the banks, so I'd say it was done by the same person. We didn't find any evidence there, so we probably won't find any evidence here, either."

"Well, I still think whoever committed these crimes lives in town," Chief Douglas said.

"Today's the last day of the month. The robber knew there was going to be a lot of money in the banks for people to cash their payroll checks."

He looked over at Principal Jenkins. "But why would he want to rob *this* safe?"

Principal Jenkins told Chief Douglas about the PTA fund raiser money that would normally have been in it. "Whoever robbed us probably knew that," she added.

Chief Douglas nodded. "Well, I can tell you one thing for sure, ladies!" he said. In a louder voice, he added, "I'm going to solve this crime—and without anybody's help, either!"

"Come on, Todd. Let's get out of here," Noelle whispered. "I think Chief Douglas knows we're eavesdropping."

"We'll never be able to *show* Chief Douglas that we know how to solve crimes, Noelle, if he won't let us near the crime scene," Todd said as they headed to their classroom.

"Don't be too sure about that, Todd," Noelle said. "We already have a couple of clues."

"We do?" Todd asked.

Noelle nodded. "The police think that the person who robbed Principal Jenkins's safe is the same person who robbed the banks," she said, "and they think that whoever it is lives right here in town."

When Noelle and Todd got to their class, Noelle told Mr. Merlin about the safe in the principal's office.

The Third-Grade Detectives were really excited. "Since the robbery was committed in our school, the police will probably expect us to solve it," Amber Lee said.

"Maybe not," Todd said.

"What do you mean?" Misty Goforth asked.

Noelle told everyone what Chief Douglas had said to them at the bank Saturday morning.

"He also told us we shouldn't be in the principal's office because it was a crime scene," Todd added.

Noelle noticed that Mr. Merlin looked upset, but he didn't say anything.

"What are we going to do, Mr. Merlin?" Amber Lee asked. "Can't we be the Third-Grade Detectives anymore?"

"Of course you can," Mr. Merlin told them. He looked at Noelle. "I'm sure you'll figure out a way to find some evidence."

Noelle grinned at him and nodded.

"I saw several of you at the blood drive on Saturday," Mr. Merlin said. "So I've decided that tomorrow, we're going to learn more about blood."

Noelle looked over at Todd.

He had turned pale.

Noelle raised her hand.

"Yes, Noelle?" Mr. Merlin said.

"Can people get sick just by listening to people *talk* about blood?" Noelle said.

Todd slumped down in his seat.

"Some people can, Noelle," Mr. Merlin said. "It's called *hemophobia*. It's not all that uncommon."

Todd straightened up. "Could we talk about that, too?" he asked.

"Of course," Mr. Merlin said.

For the rest of the morning the class wrote letters to several of their favorite authors.

When the recess bell rang, Todd started toward the playground, but Noelle pulled him back. "I have an idea," she said.

Todd followed Noelle to the cafeteria.

Mrs. Caruthers, Noelle's former baby-sitter, worked there.

"Could you give me one of those little plastic storage bags?" Noelle asked her.

"Certainly," Mrs. Caruthers said.

Outside the cafeteria, Todd asked, "What do you need that for?"

"You'll see when we get to Principal Jenkins's office," Noelle said.

They found Mrs. Franklin typing a letter.

"Are the police gone?" Noelle asked her.

Mrs. Franklin looked up and nodded.

"Did they find any evidence?" Noelle said.

"Nope. Nothing," Mrs. Franklin said.

"I even showed Chief Douglas the handkerchief I found on the floor, but he said that since it had no initials or other identifying marks, it wasn't any use to him.

"But he still thinks that whoever robbed the banks also robbed Principal Jenkins's office."

Noelle could see through the open door that Principal Jenkins was gone.

"Do you mind if Todd and I look around?" she said. "We want to see if *we* can find some clues."

"I don't mind at all. Chief Douglas makes me so mad," Mrs. Franklin said. "You Third-Grade Detectives probably know more about solving crimes than he does."

Noelle and Todd went into Principal Jenkins's office.

Noelle headed straight for the wastebasket.

She reached in, picked up the white handkerchief by a corner, and put it inside the plastic bag.

"What are you doing?" Todd asked.

"I think I'm collecting evidence," Noelle said.

Chapter Five

"Hey! Where were you and Todd?" Leon asked Noelle when everyone was back in the room after recess. "We needed two more people for kick ball."

"We didn't have time," Noelle said. "We were too busy trying to solve the mystery of who stole the second graders' pennies."

"If we can do that, we can also solve the bank robberies," Todd said.

Just then Amber Lee and Misty walked up. "Where were you two?" Amber Lee said. "We needed . . . what's in that plastic bag?"

"I think it's evidence," Noelle said. "It was—"

"All right, class, recess is over," Mr. Merlin said. "You need to sit down."

When everyone was seated, Amber Lee raised her hand.

"Yes, Amber Lee?" Mr. Merlin said.

"Noelle and Todd didn't play kick ball during recess," Amber Lee said. "They were trying to solve the mystery."

"Really?" Mr. Merlin said. He looked at Noelle.

Noelle stood up. Sometimes Amber Lee made her so mad.

"I was going to tell the class what we did, Mr. Merlin," Noelle said. She gave Amber Lee a dirty look.

"Okay, Noelle," Mr. Merlin said. "What did you and Todd do?"

Noelle told the class about the handkerchief.

"It was on the floor in Principal Jenkins's office when she discovered the robbery," Noelle said. "Mrs. Franklin threw it into the trash can before Chief Douglas and Deputy Rice got there."

"Oh, I see," Mr. Merlin said. "Did she mention it to them?"

"Yes," Noelle said. "Chief Douglas wasn't interested."

"He said it wouldn't help them solve the crime," Todd added.

"But Todd and I think the person who robbed

31

the safe may have left it," Noelle said. "We think it might be evidence."

"Good work. It certainly could be," Mr. Merlin said. "In fact, I'm going to give you a secret code clue to get you started. If you can help Chief Douglas solve this crime, it will prove to him how good the Third-Grade Detectives are."

Noelle grinned at Todd. That was exactly what she hoped they could do.

Mr. Merlin used to be a spy. He gave the class secret code clues to help them solve mysteries. He said that solving secret codes helped improve their brains.

Noelle thought he was right. She was sure her brain was better in the third grade than it had been in the second grade.

Mr. Merlin walked to the chalkboard. He wrote:

T	H	R	C	F	A
E	N	E	E	H	E
H	B	O	H	K	I
I	T	L	D	A	D
F	N	D	O	O	N

"Since it's important that we solve this crime as fast as possible, we're going to spend the rest of the day working on the secret code clue," Mr. Merlin said.

Todd leaned over to Noelle and whispered, "I think Mr. Merlin is really mad about how Chief Douglas is treating us. He's never said that before."

"I know," Noelle said.

Everyone in the class started working on the secret code clue.

Mr. Merlin never repeated the codes he gave them, but Noelle and Todd thought he might sometimes use variations of the codes.

They tried the circle code.

They tired the split alphabet code.

They tried the rail fence code.

Nothing seemed to work.

"He has to run out of new codes after a while," Todd said.

But Noelle wasn't sure that Mr. Merlin ever would. If you were a good spy, you probably had lots of secret codes, Noelle decided, and Mr. Merlin must have been a really great spy.

Noelle looked at the clock on the wall above the chalkboard. It was almost time for school to be out.

If the Third-Grade Detectives had trouble with a secret code clue, Mr. Merlin would always give them a hint to help solve it.

Noelle raised her hand.

"Okay, I'll give you a hint," Mr. Merlin said.

Noelle looked at Todd. "I didn't even have to ask him," she whispered. "He's never helped us this much—and this fast—before."

"I know," Todd agreed.

"Pretend you're looking at the Leaning Tower of Pisa," Mr. Merlin said, "but don't look at it the right way."

Just then the bell rang.

Everyone lined up at the door to leave.

Outside, some of the Third-Grade Detectives gathered around Noelle and Todd.

"Mr. Merlin's hints are harder than the secret codes," Misty complained.

"Hey! Look at me," Leon said. He was leaning to the right. "I'm the Leaning Tower of Pisa."

The Third-Grade Detectives looked at him.

"Don't be silly, Leon," Amber Lee said. "This is serious."

"No! No! No! That's it!" Noelle said. "Now I know how to decode this clue!"

Chapter Six

"Show us!" Misty said.

Noelle had an idea. She found a chalky rock on the ground.

"Stand back," she said.

She sat down on the sidewalk.

She wrote out the secret code clue in big chalky letters:

T	H	R	C	F	A
E	N	E	E	H	E
H	B	O	H	K	I
I	T	L	D	A	D
F	N	D	O	O	N

"Mr. Merlin's hint said we should pretend that we're looking at the Leaning Tower of Pisa," she said, "but that we're not supposed to look at it the *right* way."

Amber Lee rolled her eyes. "We know that, Noelle," she said, "but how do you look at it the *wrong* way?"

"Well, one opposite of right is wrong," Noelle explained, "but another opposite of right is *left*."

"Oh yeah!" Leon said. He switched from right to left. "Now the tower is leaning the other way."

"If you look at the secret code clue and lean to the left, you can solve it," Noelle said.

All of the Third-Grade Detectives leaned to the left.

"I still don't see it," Misty said.

"You will if you try to picture five Towers of Pisa leaning to the left," Noelle said.

"You start with *F*, then you go up to *I*, and then down to *N*.

"That forms the top and a side of the first tower."

"Now I see it!" Todd said. "It's a *left diagonal* clue!

"You draw a line from *D*, through *T*, to *H* and that forms one side of the *second* tower.

"A line from *H* up to *E* forms the top, and a line from *E* down to the bottom *O* forms the other side.

"Now it *really* looks like a tower!"

"Right," Noelle said. "You keep doing the rest of the code the same way."

"So the beginning of the secret code clue is *FIND THE BLO . . . ,*" Amber Lee said. "Let's hurry up and finish!"

Together, the Third-Grade Detectives solved the rest of the secret code clue: "FIND THE BLOOD ON THE HANDKERCHIEF."

"We've solved the mystery!" Leon shouted.

Todd and Noelle looked at each other.

"What's wrong?" Amber Lee said.

Noelle opened her backpack and pulled out the plastic evidence bag.

She showed it to everyone.

"There's no blood on the handkerchief," she said.

"Mr. Merlin has given us a clue that doesn't mean anything," Amber Lee complained. "Now we'll never be able to prove to Chief Douglas how good we are."

"I know," Noelle said.

"Mr. Merlin knows how important it is that we solve this mystery before the police," Todd said. "Why would he do something like this?"

Noelle shrugged. "I don't know," she said.

Chapter Seven

The next morning in class, Noelle said, "We solved the secret code clue, Mr. Merlin, but it doesn't make any sense."

"You must have made a mistake, Mr. Merlin," Leon said. "That handkerchief doesn't have any blood on it."

"We need a better secret code clue, Mr. Merlin," Amber Lee said. "We could solve the crime if you gave us a new one."

Mr. Merlin smiled. "Well, Amber Lee, I think the Third-Grade Detectives can still solve this crime if they know more about blood, and, as I said, that's exactly what we're going to study today."

Noelle looked over at Todd.

He had hemophobia, she knew. *If Todd is*

afraid of blood, how long will he be able to listen to Mr. Merlin talk about it? Noelle wondered.

"Blood flows through vessels called the circulatory system," Mr. Merlin began. "It provides food for the body.

"Half of our blood is made up of a liquid called plasma. Plasma helps the cells in the body work properly.

"The rest of the blood is made up of red blood cells, white blood cells, and platelets. Red blood cells carry oxygen from the lungs to every cell in your body.

"White blood cells fight the germs that get into your body.

"Platelets act like a plug when you get a cut.

"There are four types of blood." Mr. Merlin walked to the chalkboard. He wrote *A, B, AB,* and *O.*

"Each type can be either positive or negative, depending on whether it contains certain things called *antigens,*" he continued.

"Blood typing is very important. If a person loses a lot of blood, he or she may need a blood transfusion to replace it.

"Each person has just one type of blood in his or her body. Some types of blood work together. Other types don't.

"So when someone needs blood, because of an operation or an accident, it's very important that he or she gets the right *type* of blood.

"If a person gets the wrong blood type, then he or she could die.

"The most common blood type is A positive. The rarest type of blood is AB negative."

Noelle looked over at Todd. His face was really pale.

Noelle was enjoying hearing about blood, but she hoped Mr. Merlin was almost finished. She didn't think Todd could listen to much more of what Mr. Merlin had to say.

"The study of blood and other body fluids is called *serology*.

"Eighty percent of Americans are called *secretors*. That means their blood can also be typed by using tears, perspiration, or saliva."

Todd raised his hand.

"Yes, Todd?" Mr. Merlin said.

"May I be excused?" Todd said. "I don't feel well."

"Well, I was going to talk about hemophobia," Mr. Merlin said. "I thought you wanted to know more about that."

Todd managed to shake his head before he ran out of the room.

"I'll go see if he's all right, Mr. Merlin," Noelle said.

"Okay," Mr. Merlin said.

Noelle found Todd at the water fountain.

"I'm sorry, Noelle," Todd said. "If we don't solve this mystery, it'll be my fault. But I just couldn't listen to Mr. Merlin talk about blood anymore. You should have stayed to hear what else he had to say."

Noelle gave him a big grin.

"Don't worry, Todd. We'll solve this mystery all right," Noelle told him. "Mr. Merlin told us exactly what we needed to hear!"

Chapter Eight

The lunch bell rang while Noelle and Todd were still at the water fountain.

"I'm feeling better now," Todd said, wiping his mouth with his sleeve, "so it's all right for you to tell me what Mr. Merlin said that will help us solve the mystery."

"Well, since Mr. Merlin likes us to work together, why don't we go on to the cafeteria so I can tell the rest of the Third-Grade Detectives too," Noelle said.

"Okay," Todd said. "I just hope nobody makes fun of me because I have hemophobia."

"Don't worry about that, Todd," Noelle said. "When they hear what I have to tell them, they'll be too interested in solving this mystery to care about you."

Todd looked hurt.

"Oh, Todd, you know what I mean," Noelle said. "Everyone wants to prove to Chief Douglas how good the Third-Grade Detectives are."

Todd took another drink of water. "Okay," he said.

Most of the Third-Grade Detectives were already at the table where they all usually ate. It was at the back of the cafeteria. No one else ever sat there. Everybody in school knew this was where the Third-Grade Detectives solved a lot of mysteries.

Noelle remembered when a smart-aleck new fifth grader tried to eat there once. The other fifth graders made him move.

"Do you have hemophobia?" Amber Lee shouted, as Noelle and Todd headed toward the table. She turned to the rest of the Third-Grade Detectives. "That's when you're afraid of blood. You can't even listen to people talk about it."

Amber Lee turned back to Todd. "Is that what you have?" she shouted again.

Now the rest of the Third-Grade Detectives were looking straight at Todd.

Todd gulped.

He opened his mouth to say something, but instead Noelle said, "Todd and I know how to solve this mystery!" She smiled at everyone and sat down at the table.

Todd took the seat next to her.

"How?" Leon asked.

Before Noelle could answer, Amber Lee jumped up. "You two had this planned, didn't you?" she said. "You left the room so you wouldn't have to share what you found out with the rest of the class!"

"No, we didn't, Amber Lee," Todd said. "We . . ." He looked at Noelle and shrugged. "Yes! I have hemophobia! I'm afraid of blood," he admitted. "You can make fun of me if you want to, but we didn't leave the room so we could solve the mystery on our own. You know that Mr. Merlin likes us to work together."

"Oh, Todd, I think it's wonderful that you have hemophobia!" Amber Lee said. She sat back down. "I have alektorophobia!"

"Alektorophobia?" Noelle said. She took a bite of macaroni and cheese. "What in the world is that?"

"It's a fear of chickens," Amber Lee said. "I didn't even know I had it until last year, when we visited my uncle's chicken farm. It was a horrible experience."

"You guys are so lucky," Leon said. "I only have bibliophobia."

"What's that?" Noelle said.

"My mom says it's a fear of books," Leon said.

Good grief! Noelle thought. "Can we just—," she started to say.

But Amber Lee said, "Todd, we need to talk about this some more. I know you have arachno-phobia, too." Amber Lee turned to the rest of the Third-Grade Detectives. "That means Todd is afraid of spiders."

Todd blushed.

"There are probably a lot of other things that you and I are both afraid of," Amber Lee said. She gave Todd a big smile. "We could even start another club!"

"Well, okay, if you want to, Amber Lee,"

Todd said, "but I don't think that this is—"

"I have blennophobia. That's a fear of slime," JoAnn Dickens said. "I hate anything that's slimy!"

"My mother says I have mageirocophobia," Misty Goforth said. "That's a fear of cooking. I never want to help my mother in the kitchen."

"The mystery, everybody?" Noelle reminded them. "We need to do something about this!"

But Noelle suddenly wondered if there was something wrong with her. Was she the only Third-Grade Detective who wasn't afraid of anything?

"Tell us what you found out, Noelle," JoAnn said.

"Well, Mr. Merlin's secret code clue said that we should look for blood on the handkerchief," Noelle said.

"But there wasn't any blood on the handkerchief," Misty reminded her. "You showed it to us."

"You're right. There wasn't any *blood*," Noelle said.

"But when Mr. Merlin was talking to us, he

said that sometimes blood could be typed by other body fluids, like tears, saliva, and perspiration.

"You know how hot it is in Principal Jenkins's office. Chief Douglas and Deputy Rice were both sweating a lot.

"When the robber was trying to open the safe, he was probably sweating a lot too. He could have used the handkerchief to wipe the perspiration off his face."

"How do we really know that the handkerchief belongs to the robber?" JoAnn asked. "Couldn't it belong to somebody else?"

"I thought about that, too, JoAnn," Noelle said. "But Principal Jenkins is a very neat person. She wouldn't leave a dirty handkerchief on the floor in her office.

"And the janitors don't work on Friday nights, so they couldn't have dropped it, either.

"I really believe the only person who could have left the handkerchief there is the robber.

"And if he's a secretor, we can type his blood from the perspiration on it!"

"Dr. Smiley will help us find out for sure!" Amber Lee said. "We can use her laboratory after school! I'll go call her now."

"We may know who the robber is by tonight!" Noelle said. "That'll prove to Chief Douglas that he needs the Third-Grade Detectives to help him solve his cases!"

Chapter Nine

After school the Third-Grade Detectives headed to Dr. Smiley's house.

Just as they rounded a corner, Dr. Smiley was driving down the street from the opposite direction.

She honked her horn when she saw them.

"I hope she has lots of cookies and ice cream," Leon said. "That's what I usually eat when I get home from school."

"She always does," Todd said.

Noelle knew that Dr. Smiley didn't spend a lot of time in the kitchen. She bought her cookies from a local bakery. Noelle suddenly wondered if Dr. Smiley had mageirocophobia too.

"Hello, everybody!" Dr. Smiley said as she got

out of the car and headed to her front porch.

"May I carry your briefcase?" Amber Lee asked.

"If you want to, Amber Lee," Dr. Smiley said. "That'll free my hands to unlock the front door."

Everyone followed Dr. Smiley inside.

Noelle knew what Amber Lee was going to do next. Instead of putting the briefcase down, she went to the hall, where there was a full-length mirror. She paraded back and forth in front of it, admiring the briefcase in her hands.

"This is the type of briefcase I'm going to get for myself when I start to work for Dr. Smiley," Amber Lee said. "It goes very well with my outfit."

Noelle decided not to tell Amber Lee that by the time Dr. Smiley asked her to work for her, that outfit would be too small.

After Dr. Smiley served everyone snacks, they went downstairs to her laboratory.

Noelle handed her the plastic bag with the white handkerchief.

"If the person who robbed the safe in Principal Jenkins's office used this handkerchief to wipe off perspiration, then we can test it for proteins and enzymes," Dr. Smiley said.

"If the person is a secretor, then I'll be able to type his or her blood.

"These days, DNA technology has replaced the test for specific types of proteins and enzymes, but those tests can only be done in a bigger laboratory, such as the one at the state police headquarters."

The Third-Grade Detectives gathered around Dr. Smiley's laboratory table.

Dr. Smiley put a piece of paper treated with starch over the handkerchief and wet it down.

"This paper will absorb the enzymes and proteins," she said.

After several minutes Dr. Smiley sprayed the paper with a chemical.

Some big blue blobs appeared.

"These blue spots are the person's perspiration," Dr. Smiley told them. "If he or she is a secretor, then this next test will tell me what type of blood the person has."

Noelle held her breath.

The future of the Third-Grade Detectives was at stake.

Finally Dr. Smiley said, "Perfect! The person who left this handkerchief in Principal Jenkins's office is a secretor. His or her blood type is AB negative. We're in luck. That's the rarest blood type there is."

"Who was it?" Leon asked.

"Unfortunately we don't have a name to go with the blood type," Dr. Smiley said.

Just then the doorbell rang.

"Will somebody get that?" Dr. Smiley said. "It's probably Mr. Merlin. I asked him to come over."

Noelle and Todd hurried up the basement steps.

When they opened the front door, Mr. Merlin was standing outside.

"The person who left the handkerchief in Principal Jenkins's office has the rarest type of blood there is," Noelle said.

"But we don't know a name, so what good is that going to do us?"

"We need another secret code clue, Mr. Merlin," Todd said.

Mr. Merlin smiled. "With the information that Dr. Smiley just gave you, I have the perfect clue for you!"

When they got downstairs, Mr. Merlin went to Dr. Smiley's small chalkboard, erased some notes, and wrote:

H	T	E	V	H	W
R	E	T	B	A	O
I	D	B	A	L	G
B	V	D	L	D	O
C	A	E	O	O	O

Noelle thought the code might be another type of diagonal, but they didn't have any time to waste, so she said, "Would you give us another hint now?"

"Well, I don't plan to make a habit of giving you hints right after I give you a secret code clue, because I like for you to use your brains," Mr. Merlin said, "but I want you to prove to Chief Douglas as soon as possible that the Third-Grade

Detectives can help the police solve mysteries."

The Third-Grade Detectives cheered.

"So here's a hint," Mr. Merlin said. "The Towers of Pisa still lean to the left, but now you have to read them right."

Chapter Ten

Noelle remembered how she had started on the *bottom left-hand side* of the first secret code clue. She had to do that to make sure she had leaning towers.

So if the towers still leaned to the left, but you had to read it *right*, that probably meant you should start on the *top right-hand side* this time.

"I think I have it, Todd," Noelle whispered.

The rest of the Third-Grade Detectives were sitting on the floor of Dr. Smiley's laboratory. They were all trying to solve the secret code clue.

Everyone knew that Mr. Merlin liked them to work together to solve the mystery, but he didn't mind if they had a contest to see who solved the secret code clue first.

Noelle started at the upper right-hand corner

of the secret code clue with *W*. She drew a line to *H*, which made the top of the first tower, then she drew a line from *H* to *O* to form the side. "The first word in the clue is *Who*," she whispered to Todd.

Together, Noelle and Todd made towers leaning to the left through the entire code.

"*Who gave blood at the blood drive* plus *A*, *B*, and *C* to finish out the square," Todd said.

"Of course! My parents told me that almost everybody in town gave blood," Noelle said. "The police think the robber is someone local, so that's where we need to start looking for a person with AB negative blood."

Noelle started to raise her hand, but Amber Lee beat her to it.

"*Who gave blood at the blood drive!*" Amber Lee shouted. She grinned at Noelle.

"That's right, Amber Lee," Mr. Merlin said.

Noelle wanted to tell Mr. Merlin that she and Todd had solved it too, but there were more important things to do.

She raised her hand.

"Yes, Noelle?" Mr. Merlin said.

"I can call my parents. They have a list of all of the people who gave blood," Noelle said. "They may know who has type AB negative."

"That's a good idea, Noelle," Mr. Merlin said.

Noelle's mother answered the telephone.

"We just have the *names* of the people who donated blood," Mrs. Trocoderro told her. "The blood bank would have each person's blood type, but that might be private information."

"But it's important that we know, Mom, so we can solve the mystery of who robbed the banks and Principal Jenkins's safe," Noelle said.

"Well, I guess you could call them," Mrs. Trocoderro said. "Since it's to solve a crime, they might be willing to help."

"The robber has type AB negative blood," Noelle said. "That's the rarest—"

"Oh, my goodness! How terrible!" Mrs. Trocoderro said. "I can't believe that!"

"What do you mean, Mom?" Noelle said.

"Well, everybody at the blood drive was talking about it," Mrs. Trocoderro said. "The only person in town who is AB negative is Mr. Polk, our insurance man!"

Noelle couldn't believe it either. Mr. Polk seemed like such a nice man.

Noelle hung up the receiver and told everyone what her mother had said.

"Oh, no!" Dr. Smiley said. "He's my insurance man too."

"He's also my insurance man," Mr. Merlin said. "There must be some mistake."

"Science doesn't lie," Dr. Smiley finally said. "The blood type of the perspiration on that handkerchief is AB negative."

Dr. Smiley went to the telephone and called Chief Douglas. She told him what the Third-Grade Detectives had discovered. She talked to him in a soft voice for several minutes. Finally she hung up the receiver.

"Unfortunately Chief Douglas still doesn't want to believe that the Third-Grade Detectives might have solved this crime," Dr. Smiley said, "but he's agreed to talk to Mr. Polk."

Nobody cheered.

Nobody could believe that Mr. Polk might have robbed the banks and stolen the second graders' pennies.

The next morning, when the Third-Grade Detectives returned from recess, Dr. Smiley and Chief Douglas were standing at the front of the room with Mr. Merlin.

"Chief Douglas wants to say something to you," Mr. Merlin told them when everyone was seated.

Chief Douglas cleared his throat. Noelle thought he looked really nervous.

"I want to apologize to the Third-Grade Detectives. I was wrong about you," Chief Douglas said. "You solved this crime, and I really appreciate your work. Mr. Polk admitted that he robbed the banks, and that he even stole the pennies from Principal Jenkins's safe because he was mad that the PTA fund raiser money wasn't there."

"What was he going to do with all that money?" Noelle asked.

"Move to Hawaii," Chief Douglas said. "He told me he was tired of selling insurance."

That's sad, Noelle thought. She'd miss seeing Mr. Polk at their house.

"The police are also having trouble solving another crime," Chief Douglas said. "Would you be interested in helping us with it?"

"Yes!" the Third-Grade Detectives shouted.

Dr. Smiley grinned at Todd and Noelle.

Noelle was happy.

Things were finally back to normal again.

State Secret

Can you find the secret message that's in the shape of a big state?

```
J  A  O  T  H  I  S  C  R  K  K  V
K  B  P  A  I  J  I  D  S  L  L  W
L  C  Q  S  J  K  S  E  T  M  M  X
M  D  R  A  K  L  A  F  U  N  N  Y
N  E  S  X  L  M  B  G  V  O  O  S
O  F  T  E  M  N  C  H  W  P  P  E
P  E  U  F  N  O  D  I  X  Q  Q  C
Q  P  V  G  S  P  E  J  Y  R  E  R
R  Q  A  H  T  E  F  K  Z  C  T  S
S  R  B  I  U  F  H  L  D  O  U  T
T  S  C  J  V  G  I  T  E  P  V  U
U  T  D  K  W  H  J  N  I  Q  W  V
```

1st hint: This state is called the Lone Star State. Can you find it now?

2nd hint: The capital of this state is Austin. Can you find it now?

3rd hint: If you still can't find it, look for the message: THIS IS A FUNNY SECRET CODE IN THE SHAPE OF TEXAS. If you circle or highlight the letters of these words, you'll see the shape of Texas. (Hint: Look at the first line of the secret code to find the first word of the message!)

You can make a secret code out of your own state. Here's how to do it:

1. Find a map of your state in a book or a magazine and make a photocopy of it. Be sure to reduce it so that it will fit into a secret code about the size of the one above. (Remember, too, that the shapes of some states are more recognizable than others!)

2. Trace around the edges of the state with a dark marker.

3. Put a piece of 1/4 inch graph paper over the state.

4. Write your secret message in the graph squares that follow the outline of your state. (You may not be able to make every curve in your state perfect, but just do the best you can!)

5. Make sure that your secret message isn't longer than the number of graph squares that you have available.

6. If you don't need all of your graph squares for the secret message, then just use as many alphabet letters as you need to finish filling out the rest of the outline of your state.

7. Finally, fill in the squares around your secret message with other letters of the alphabet, so that you'll have a square (or a rectangle). It's best to do the letters consecutively. (Look at the letters that are filled in around the Texas secret message square to see how this is done.)

THIRD-GRADE DETECTIVES

Everyone in the third grade loves the new teacher, Mr. Merlin.

Mr. Merlin used to be a spy, and he knows all about secret codes and the strange and gross ways the police solve mysteries.

YOU CAN HELP DECODE THE CLUES AND SOLVE THE MYSTERY IN THESE OTHER STORIES ABOUT THE THIRD-GRADE DETECTIVES:

#1 **The Clue of the Left-handed Envelope**

#2 **The Puzzle of the Pretty Pink Handkerchief**

#3 **The Mystery of the Hairy Tomatoes**

#4 **The Cobweb Confession**

#5 **The Riddle of the Stolen Sand**

#6 **The Secret of the Green Skin**

#7 **The Case of the Dirty Clue**

#8 **The Secret of the Wooden Witness**

#9 **The Case of the Sweaty Bank Robber**

Coming Soon: #10 The Mystery of the Stolen Statue

When **GEORGE E. STANLEY** was in the third grade, he dreamed that he helped Nancy Drew and the Hardy Boys solve a very important mystery. After the case was closed, Nancy, Frank, and Joe told George that if it hadn't been for him, their crime-solving days would probably have been over! Right before he woke up, they made George promise that he would become either a famous detective or a famous writer of detective stories. Over the years George has written many, many books for young readers, but it is only now, with the Third-Grade Detectives, that he has finally fulfilled his promise to his good friends.

When not dreaming of Nancy Drew and the Hardy Boys or writing for young readers, George E. Stanley is a professor of languages and linguistics at Cameron University, where he also teaches courses in children's literature. He lives in Lawton, Oklahoma.

SALVATORE MURDOCCA has illustrated numerous picture books as well as the best-selling chapter book series The Magic Treehouse. He lives in New City, New York.